PIGS IN HIDING

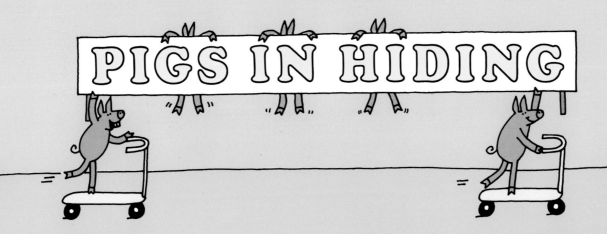

PIGS IN HIDING

Arlene Dubanevich

FOUR WINDS PRESS
New York

10 9 8 7 6 5 4 3
The text of this book is hand-lettered by the artist.
The illustrations are black line drawings with overlays,
prepared by the artist for black, red, yellow, and blue.
Library of Congress Cataloging in Publication Data
Dubanevich, Arlene.
Pigs in hiding.
Summary: A game of hide-and-seek played
by a number of pigs allows the reader to find
the animals in their hiding places.
[1. Hide-and-seek—Fiction.   2. Pigs—Fiction]
I. Title.   PZ7.D8492Pi   1983   [E]   83-1409
ISBN 0-590-07872-0

To Mom

The End.